LONG LIVE EARTH

LONG LIVE EARTH

Meighan Morrison

SCHOLASTIC INC.
NEW YORK TORONTO LONDON AUCKLAND SYDNEY

ISBN 0-590-48012-X

Copyright © 1993 by Meighan Morrison. All rights reserved. Published by Scholastic Inc., 555 Broadway, New York, NY 10012, by arrangement with Ashton Scholastic.

13 12 11 10 9 8 7 6 5 4 3 2   4 5 6 7 8 9/9

Printed in the U.S.A.   14

First Scholastic printing, April 1994

A Note from the Author

Thank you for selecting this book. Thank you for caring about the future of our planet and of our children.

I believe that a person's basic values and sense of right and wrong are formed in the very early years of life. Parents may need to explain the meaning of some words in the text and expand on certain parts, but if this book can provide even one child with the knowledge and encouragement needed to become involved in the preservation of our environment, then it has been worthwhile.

My generation and those before it have endangered our planet, but it is up to our children and their children to save it. Children are our greatest resource. They are the hope for the future of the earth.

Long live our children!

For Benjamin

arth once spun in space,
a great, seething ball,
long before it became
a home to us all.

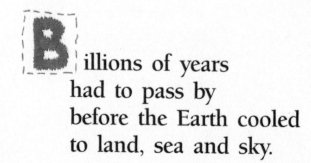illions of years
had to pass by
before the Earth cooled
to land, sea and sky.

hen millions more years
till the first plants and trees
and small living beings
crawled from the seas.

Dinosaurs lived here
with other huge creatures,
well before Early Man
with his ape-like features.

The Earth sustained life
since life first began;
all plants and all creatures
in union with Man.

The environment gave
what living things need:
clean air, clean water,
warmth, shelter and feed.

But parts of all nations
have now been abused —
Earth has been poisoned,
plundered and used.

This terrible truth
brings, to all people, shame.
We cause the damage.
Ours is the blame.

We chop down the trees
that keep the air clean.
The birds are left homeless . . .
some no longer seen.

ast forests are milled
for buildings and papers,
and fertile green land
is used for skyscrapers.

 xhaust fumes and vapors
clothe cities in smog.
This is air thick with dirt –
not a harmless gray fog.

e poison Earth's bounty
with chemical spray
and leave mountains of waste
to pollute and decay.

In places, sea life
can barely survive.
In very bad water
there's nothing alive.

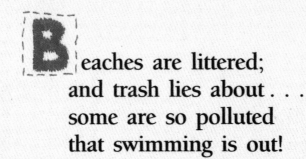

eaches are littered;
and trash lies about . . .
some are so polluted
that swimming is out!

This magnificent Earth
deserves far better care.
We can help in its rescue
if we each do our share.

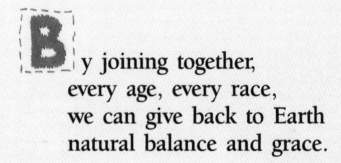

By joining together,
every age, every race,
we can give back to Earth
natural balance and grace.

ave precious resources.
Don't throw things away!
So much can be salvaged
for recycling each day.

Using both sides of paper
to paint on, or draw,
can save a whole tree
from an axe or a saw.

Think of walking or biking
before using the car.
Take the bus or the train
if you have to go far.

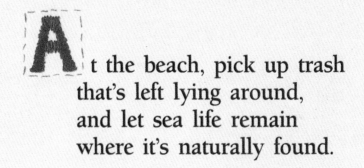

At the beach, pick up trash
that's left lying around,
and let sea life remain
where it's naturally found.

If you can, plant a tree
or a garden to suit.
Be good to the soil,
and the seed will bear fruit.

ven one small green plant
will help cleanse the air;
indoors or outdoors –
it helps anywhere.

ell Mayors, Prime Ministers,
Presidents, too,
how very important
the Earth is to you.

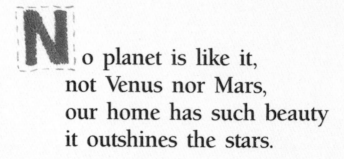

No planet is like it,
not Venus nor Mars,
our home has such beauty
it outshines the stars.

reat it with thoughtfulness.
Treasure its worth.
Tend it with loving . . .

Long live the Earth!